The Road to Hana

By Larry N. Gerston

Illustrated by Gary Beattie

Requests for permission to make copies of any part of this work should be mailed to Permissions Department, Llumina Press, 7580 NW 5th Street 16535 Plantation, FL 33318.

ISBN: 978-1-62550-255-1

　　　978-1-62550-256-8

　　　978-1-62550-257-5

Printed in the United States of America by Llumina Press

Library of Congress Control Number: 2015915402

WITH THANKS TO GORDON

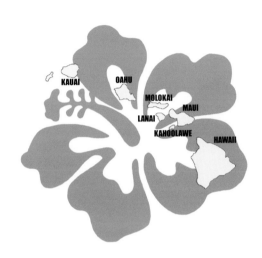

ACKNOWLEDGEMENTS

Every book comes into print with the help of many along the way. The author wishes to thank Deborah Greenspan, Publisher and Shari Reimann, Production Coordinator at Llumina for their careful care of the project. Special thanks go to Elisa Gerston, spouse and in-house editor extraordinaire.

Gia Gabriella awakened full of excitement. She was in Maui, an island in beautiful Hawai'i, for the first time with her Aunt Rachel and Uncle Lee. Today, they would take her to Hana, a sleepy town on the other side of Maui. There would be lots to see along the way.

Gia knew it would take a long time to drive to Hana. The 40-mile road to Hana has 631 curves. Sometimes the road bends so much that the car has to go as slow as a person walking next to it along the side of the road.

4

The trip would take at least four hours each way. Gia would be patient because she wanted to see everything along the route.

She wanted to see the big waves, the giant philodendron leaves that looked like elephant ears, the banana bread stand, the rare rainbow eucalyptus trees, the waterfalls, and all the beautiful things on the road to Hana.

"Are you ready to go?" Uncle Lee asked.

Gia nodded with excitement and said, "I want to see everything!"

"Don't forget, Lee," Aunt Rachel said, "We have lots to do today. I need to be back at the hotel by 3:00 before the sandal shop closes."

"Yes," Uncle Lee replied. "And I have a surfing lesson at 2:30, so we better go fast."

Gia looked at her watch. She had just learned how to tell time, and it was now 8:00.

"Oh dear," she thought. "The drive to Hana takes four hours, which means we will get there at 12:00 noon. And the drive back to the hotel takes another four hours, which means we should be back by 4:00. And that's if we don't stop along the way."

She asked Uncle Lee and Aunt Rachel, "How can we see all the wonderful things on the road to Hana if we come back so soon?"

"Oh, we'll have plenty of time," they said. But Gia wasn't so sure.

Meanwhile, Uncle Lee drove fast on the highway full of curves. Everything seemed like a blur.

"Uncle Lee, Aunt Rachel, we're going so fast that I can't see anything very well. Can we slow down?"

16

"Oh, don't worry," said Aunt Rachel, "We'll see everything when we get to Hana."

Finally, after more than three hours in the car, Uncle Lee, Aunt Rachel, and Gia arrived in Hana. They didn't stop once along the way.

18

They looked around and saw only a few deserted buildings, old railroad tracks, and a broken pier that was locked up. No one was there except a very old Hawaiian man leaning against an empty building. Uncle Lee ran up to the old man.

"Excuse me, Sir," said Uncle Lee, "is this Hana?" The old man slowly stood up. "Yes," he said slowly with a thick Hawaiian accent, "This is Hana."

Uncle Lee, Aunt Rachel, and Gia looked puzzled. "Well," Uncle Lee, asked, "where are the big waves?"

"No big waves in Hana," the old man replied.

A confused Aunt Rachel spoke up, "Where are the giant philodendron leaves?"

"No giant philodendron leaves in Hana," said the old man.

Frustrated, Gia inquired, "Well, what about the banana bread stand, the rainbow eucalyptus trees, and the waterfalls? They must be in Hana."

The old man thought for a moment, smiled, and then said, "All those things are not in Hana. Those things are on the road to Hana."

Uncle Lee was the first to talk: "Maybe we drove too fast to see anything."

Added Aunt Rachel: "I think we were in too much of a hurry."

Said Gia, "We were so busy going to Hana that we didn't see all the wonderful places on the road to Hana. We made a big mistake."

"Well," Aunt Rachel offered, "We didn't see very much on the road to Hana, but we're going to take it slow when we leave Hana."

And so on the way back to the hotel on the other side of the island, they drove slowly so they could see the sights.

Just outside of Hana, they stopped at a roadside stand for a Hawaiian barbecue lunch.

Soon after they began the drive home, they stopped and viewed the high waterfalls.

Along the way, they watched surfers on the big waves;

they picked off bark from the rare eucalyptus trees
with rainbow colored bark;

they tasted the
fresh baked banana bread;

they played hide-and-seek behind
the giant philodendron leaves;

and they visited all the other beautiful stops they didn't see on the road to Hana, including a majestic rainbow that seemed to fall into the ocean.

"There were so many wonderful things between here and Hana," said Gia. "I'm so happy we stopped to see them."

"You're right," said Uncle Lee.

Aunt Rachel added, "You know, the road between the hotel and Hana was the best part of the drive to Hana. I'm sure glad we had a chance to see everything on our way back. I'll remember that if we go again."

"Don't worry," Gia giggled. "Next time I'll drive."

44

They all laughed and sat down to look at the pictures of the beautiful sights they saw on the road to Hana.